Jamaica

BLAINE WISEMAN

MEDIA ENHANCED BOOKS
AV2 BY WEIGL
ADDED VALUE • AUDIO VISUAL

www.av2books.com

AV² provides enriched content that supplements and complements this book. Weigl's AV² books strive to create inspired learning and engage young minds in a total learning experience.

Your AV² Media Enhanced books come alive with...

Audio
Listen to sections of the book read aloud.

Key Words
Study vocabulary, and complete a matching word activity.

Video
Watch informative video clips.

Quizzes
Test your knowledge.

Embedded Weblinks
Gain additional information for research.

Slideshow
View images and captions, and prepare a presentation.

Try This!
Complete activities and hands-on experiments.

... and much, much more!

Go to **www.av2books.com**, and enter this book's unique code.

BOOK CODE

A V L 6 3 3 3 6

AV² by Weigl brings you media enhanced books that support active learning.

Published by AV² by Weigl
350 5th Avenue, 59th Floor
New York, NY 10118
Website: www.av2books.com

Library of Congress Control Number: 2019938449

ISBN 978-1-7911-0910-3 (hardcover)
ISBN 978-1-7911-0911-0 (softcover)
ISBN 978-1-7911-0912-7 (multi-user eBook)
ISBN 978-1-7911-0913-4 (single-user eBook)

Printed in Guangzhou, China
1 2 3 4 5 6 7 8 9 0 23 22 21 20 19

062019
311018

Editor Heather Kissock
Art Director Terry Paulhus
Layout Tammy West

Photo Credits
Every reasonable effort has been made to trace ownership and to obtain permission to reprint copyright material. The publishers would be pleased to have any errors or omissions brought to their attention so that they may be corrected in subsequent printings.

Weigl acknowledges Getty Images, Alamy, iStock, and Shutterstock as its primary photo suppliers for this title.

Contents

Jamaica Overview

Jamaica is an island country located in the Caribbean Sea. Once a European **colony**, Jamaica's history has been shaped by its struggle for freedom. Today, this independent spirit can still be seen in the Jamaican people, who have worked hard to maintain and promote the island's vibrant culture and easy-going nature. Tourists come to Jamaica to relax and experience the island's scenic beauty. The country is more than a tourist destination, however. Jamaica also produces goods that are in demand globally. Crops such as sugarcane, bananas, and coffee beans are shipped to consumers around the world.

Jamaica is a popular stop for cruise ships traveling through the Caribbean. Cruise ships make more than 440 stops at Jamaican ports every year.

Reminders of Jamaica's colonial past can be seen in the architecture of buildings such as Devon House, the home of the island's first black millionaire.

Jerk chicken is one of Jamaica's best-known dishes. It is flavored with a blend of herbs, spices, hot peppers, and pimento wood.

The steel drum is a uniquely Caribbean instrument. Jamaican bands often incorporate its sound into their music.

As an island nation, Jamaica has several lighthouses to guide ships. Built in 1894, the Negril Point lighthouse is one of the island's oldest.

Exploring Jamaica

J amaica is the third-largest island in the Caribbean, after Cuba and Hispaniola. It is part of the island group known as the Greater Antilles, which itself belongs to a region called the West Indies. Jamaica covers an area of 4,243 square miles (10,989 square kilometers). Its coastline stretches for 635 miles (1,022 km). Jamaica's nearest neighbors are the other islands of the Greater Antilles. Cuba is 90 miles (145 km) north of Jamaica. Hispaniola, home to Haiti and the Dominican Republic, lies 99 miles (159 km) to the east. The closest mainland point is 390 miles (628 km) away in Honduras, Central America.

Cockpit Country

Black River

N

Map Legend

Jamaica

Land

Water

▲ Blue Mountain Peak

Black River

Cockpit Country

Capital City

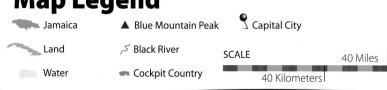
SCALE

40 Miles

40 Kilometers

Black River

The Black River runs 33 miles (53 km) through southern Jamaica. It is an important water source for the island's people. The river is named for its dark color. Rotting plants along the riverbed stain the water the color of tea.

Cuba

Caribbean Sea

Blue Mountain Peak

JAMAICA

Kingston

Kingston

Caribbean Sea

Cockpit Country

Cockpit Country is a natural area covering about 500 square miles (1,295 sq. km) in west-central Jamaica. Made up of the country's largest native forest, the area gets its name from the many **sinkholes**, or cockpits, found in the ground.

Blue Mountain Peak

Jamaica's highest point is Blue Mountain Peak, which stands 7,402 feet (2,256 meters) above sea level. Tourists often hike to the top of Blue Mountain Peak in the dark of the early morning to watch the Sun rise over the mountains.

Kingston

Kingston is Jamaica's largest city and capital. It is home to about one quarter of the country's population. Located on the southeast coast, Kingston is also Jamaica's biggest and most important port.

LAND AND CLIMATE

Jamaica is a land of mountains, **plateaus**, plains, and rivers. The island's interior is mostly made up of mountain ranges and plateaus that fall rapidly toward the coastal plains. The Blue Mountains and John Crow Mountains stretch across the eastern part of the country. The north central part of Jamaica is dominated by the Dry Harbour Mountains and Cockpit Country. Southern Jamaica is home to the Don Figuerero Mountains, the May Day Mountains, and the Santa Cruz Mountains.

The Rio Minho was called the Rio de la Mina, or River of the Mine, by the Spanish. When they first explored the island, they found traces of gold in the sand along its banks.

Rivers begin in the mountain peaks and wind through forests, rainforests, and **savannas** on their way to the coast. These waterways often disappear into limestone caves and cockpits before reappearing in other areas. Jamaica's longest river is the Rio Minho. It begins near the center of the island and flows southeast for 58 miles (92.8 km) before emptying into the Caribbean Sea.

Jamaica's climate is a product of wind and water. **Trade winds** blow in from the northeast, bringing the warm, humid, **tropical** air that makes Caribbean weather so pleasant. Cool breezes from the coastal waters give relief from the heat. In the winter, colder air arrives from the north on winds known as northers. In general, however, temperatures remain stable throughout the year. Coastal areas tend to be warmer than the interior, with daytime temperatures between 80 and 89° Fahrenheit (30 and 35° Celsius). Higher elevations can be as cold as 40°F (4°C).

The mountains also influence weather patterns on the island. The interior mountains block moisture from reaching southwestern Jamaica. As a result, the eastern side of the island receives more rainfall than the west. East Jamaica can get up to 130 inches (330 centimeters) of rain per year. The island's annual average is only 82 inches (208 cm).

In the Caribbean, there are wet and dry seasons. Jamaica's rainy seasons occur in October and May. July to September is hurricane season. While Jamaica lies to the side of the **hurricane belt**, the island has been damaged by several major storms. The most recent was Hurricane Matthew, which caused flooding along Jamaica's coast in 2016.

Land and Climate BY THE NUMBERS

2/3
Portion of Jamaica covered by limestone plateau.

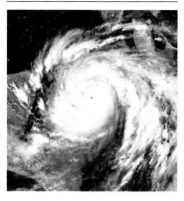

500,000 Number of Jamaicans left homeless by Hurricane Gilbert in 1988.

146 miles Length of Jamaica at its greatest extent. (235 km)

The Blue Mountains and John Crow Mountains form one of Jamaica's national parks. The Blue and John Crow Mountains National Park was named a UNESCO World Heritage Site in 2015, due in part to the many rare plants and animals that live within it.

PLANTS AND ANIMALS

45% Portion of Jamaica covered by woodland and forest.

1959 Year the Blue Mahoe was chosen as Jamaica's national tree.

28 Number of bird species found only in Jamaica.

Jamaica's lush landscape supports a wide variety of plants. In the southern part of the country, dry forests resemble desert areas, and support small trees, shrubs, and several cactus **species**. Coastal areas are ringed with **mangrove** forests. The mangroves serve an important purpose, as they protect the coastline from **erosion**.

As a tropical island, Jamaica is home to many exotic plants. Ferns are common throughout the island, as are orchids. Of the approximately 220 orchid species found in Jamaica, 66 are considered **endemic**. The sundew is another plant native to Jamaica. It uses its sticky leaves to catch the insects it eats.

Birds and bats are the most common animals found in Jamaica. The doctor bird is Jamaica's national bird. It can be found throughout the country. Another bird, the jacana, can often be seen walking on floating lily pads. Jamaica has 21 different bat species, including the native Jamaican fruit-eating bat. Whales, dolphins, sharks, turtles, and many other aquatic animals can be found in the Caribbean waters around Jamaica as well.

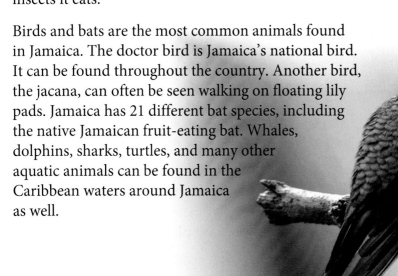

Male doctor birds are known for their long tails, which can grow to about 6 inches (15 cm).

NATURAL RESOURCES

Jamaica has an abundance of natural resources. Its climate is a key support of these resources. The warm, humid temperatures provide excellent conditions for growing fruit. Rainfall ensures that fruit gets the moisture it needs to grow. Rain also helps to keep the soil moist and nutrient rich. Oranges, bananas, and coconuts are just some of the fruits grown in Jamaica.

The waters surrounding Jamaica support abundant fish resources. About 60 miles (97 km) south of Jamaica is an area called Pedro Bank. It is the main fishing area for islanders. Snapper, lobster, grouper, and conch are some of the most commonly fished species.

Some of Jamaica's most important resources are found in the ground. **Bauxite** is present in large quantities in Jamaica. It is used to make aluminum. Marble, limestone, and gypsum are some of the other resources commonly mined on the island.

3,104 square miles
Area covered by Pedro Bank.
(8,040 sq. km)

7% Portion of the world's bauxite reserves found in Jamaica.

More than 120,000
Number of new banana trees produced in Jamaica each year.

Yams are another important crop in Jamaica. The soil in Jamaica is considered ideal for growing yams as it is deep and well-drained.

TOURISM

Jamaica is one of the most popular tourist destinations in the Caribbean. Each year, more than 4 million people visit Jamaica for its beaches, scenery, and culture. Most tourists head to resort towns such as Montego Bay, Ocho Rios, or Negril. The city of Falmouth is the main stopping point for cruise ships, where thousands of people arrive and leave each day.

White sand and clear blue water stretch for miles (km) along Jamaica's coastline. Seven Mile Beach, near Negril, is among the best known. Swimming, scuba diving, and snorkeling are popular activities. Tourists can also go whale watching, sport fishing, or swimming with dolphins.

Snorkelers have the opportunity to swim among the many creatures found in Jamaica's waters, including the sergeant major fish.

Not all of Jamaica's attractions are located along the coast. The country's rivers offer a variety of inland activities. Visitors to Montego Bay can raft along the Martha Brae River. They travel upriver on 30-foot (9-m) long bamboo rafts, steered by tour guides. On their journey, rafters learn about local culture, history, and the plants and animals found in the area.

The Martha Brae rafting tours are approximately an hour long and traverse about 3 miles (4.8 km) of the river. They are a popular tourist activity.

At Dunn's River Falls, near Ocho Rios, tourists gather to sunbathe and swim in the natural pools. Many visitors climb to the top of the falls to enjoy the scenery below. The Green Grotto Caves give visitors a chance to learn about Jamaica's natural and cultural history. Surrounded by forest and filled with clear green water, these caves have housed Jamaica's ancient peoples, served as hideouts for 17th century pirates, and played host to millions of tourists.

The capital city is another major stopping point for tourists. Kingston offers visitors a range of things to do and see. The National Gallery of Jamaica houses a large collection of art from Jamaican artists throughout the 20th century. The Natural History Museum of Jamaica displays and preserves Jamaican plants and animals, and tells the story of how Jamaica came to be. Music lovers seek out the Bob Marley Museum to learn more about Jamaica's best-known musician.

The Blue Mountains rise above the outskirts of Kingston, making them a popular day trip for tourists wanting a break from the city. There, they can spend the day hiking mountain trails or trekking to the top of Blue Mountain Peak. Visitors can also see and taste the world-renowned Blue Mountain coffee.

Tourism BY THE NUMBERS

845,652 Number of people who arrived in Falmouth by cruise ship in 2017.

$3.3 billion
Amount of money tourists spent in Jamaica in 2018 in U.S. dollars.

1879 Year the Natural History Museum of Jamaica was established.

Dunn's River Falls are terraced, forming natural stairs for visitors to climb. The falls are about 180 feet (55 m) high and about 600 feet (183 m) long.

INDUSTRY

In the past, agriculture and fishing were the most important industries in Jamaica. However, the mid-20th century saw the rise of the country's manufacturing industry. Today, agriculture, mining and manufacturing are the country's main industries.

About one in six working Jamaicans is employed in agriculture. While these workers include private farmers, most agricultural workers are employed by major corporations. Large **plantations** grow sugarcane for a variety of uses and industries. Coffee and tobacco are other crops controlled mainly by large corporations.

These crops contribute to Jamaica's manufacturing industry as well. Sugarcane is processed to make rum and molasses. It can also be burned to generate electricity. Other products manufactured in Jamaica include **textiles** and metal products.

Much of the country's mining industry focuses on the extraction and processing of bauxite. The country currently has four processing plants. Raw bauxite is also shipped to other countries, such as the United States, for processing.

1938 Year bauxite was discovered in Jamaica.

16.1% Portion of Jamaican workers employed in agriculture industry.

MORE THAN 300
Number of companies in Jamaica engaged in manufacturing activities.

Rail cars are often used to transfer bauxite from the mines to Jamaica's ports and processing plants.

GOODS AND SERVICES

T he service sector dominates the Jamaican economy, accounting for about 70 percent of the country's **gross domestic product (GDP)**. Workers in this sector provide services to others rather than produce goods. Most service jobs in Jamaica are found in tourism and financial services. Hotels are one of the largest employers in the tourism industry. Banks are the biggest driver in financial services, helping people save, spend, and move their money. One of the largest parts of this industry involves receiving **remittances** from overseas relatives.

Jamaican goods are shipped to markets all around the world. Aluminum oxide is the country's top **export** product, making up more than 40 percent of all exports. This product, which is made from bauxite, is used in the manufacturing of a variety of items, ranging from airplanes to paint. The product most commonly **imported** into Jamaica is petroleum. It helps fuel cars, and power homes and businesses. More than 50 percent of Jamaica's petroleum comes from the United States, the country's biggest trading partner.

$379 million Total value of Jamaican products exported to the United States in 2018.

50%
Approximate portion of Jamaican workers employed in the service sector.

$2.49 billion
Amount Jamaicans received in 2017 from family and friends who live abroad.

$26 BILLION
Size of Jamaica's GDP in 2017.

Most of Jamaica's export and import goods travel through the Port of Kingston. Besides being Jamaica's largest port, Kingston is one of the busiest ports in the Caribbean and Latin America.

INDIGENOUS PEOPLES

Some **archaeologists** believe the first people to live in Jamaica were known as the Ciboney. While there are no official records of these people, **oral** tradition tells of cave dwellers who lived on the island long ago. The Ciboney are known to have lived on the other islands of the Greater Antilles, arriving in the area between 5000 and 4000 BC.

In about 600 AD, a group known as the "Redware people" arrived in Jamaica. Named for the red **earthenware** associated with them, they are believed to have been a subgroup of South America's Arawak peoples. The Redware people set up communities along the island's coast and fished in the local waters.

About 200 years after the Redware people landed on the island, another group of Arawaks, known as the Taínos, arrived in Jamaica. They gave the island the name, *Xaymaca*, which means "land of wood and water." The Taíno overtook the Redware and Ciboney people, making many of them slaves.

200 Approximate number of Taíno villages once scattered throughout Jamaica.

3,000 Maximum population of a Taíno village.

6 million
Approximate number of Arawak living in the Caribbean before the arrival of the Europeans.

The Taíno were one of the most widespread indigenous groups of the Caribbean. Remains of their culture have been found on many of the islands in the region, including Puerto Rico, Cuba, Hispaniola, and Jamaica.

TAÍNO SETTLEMENT

The Taíno people formed agricultural communities on the island, growing corn, **cassava**, yams, and other crops. They also relied on the abundant **fisheries** in the area. Along with farming and fishing, the Taíno hunted for food, taking advantage of the wildlife found throughout the island.

Each Taíno village was ruled by a *cacique*, or chief. He ensured that work was assigned and completed, and that everyone was treated fairly. The cacique was also responsible for the village's defense. He made sure that his warriors were ready if the village was threatened by outsiders.

The Carib people, in particular, presented a serious threat to the Taínos. In fact, it is believed that the Taíno arrived in Jamaica because the Carib had forced them out of South America. In the 15th century, the Carib's efforts to claim more land for themselves led them to the Greater Antilles, where they once again battled with the Taíno. This struggle for control of the area led to much conflict between the two groups. Near the end of the century, however, European explorers arrived in the area, replacing this threat with another, more powerful, one.

1492
Year explorer Christopher Columbus arrived in the Caribbean.

60,000 Number of Taínos living on Jamaica in 1492.

1940s Decade in which the remains of the Taíno village of Maima were uncovered in Jamaica by archaeologist Charles Cotter.

Fish and shellfish were an important food source for the Taíno. The would eat it raw or partially cooked.

THE AGE OF EXPLORATION

Christopher Columbus first landed in Jamaica on May 5, 1494. Shortly after arriving, he claimed the island as a Spanish colony. However, it would be 15 more years until the Spanish settled the island.

The first European settlement on Jamaica was founded in 1509 by Juan de Esquivel, a member of Columbus's second voyage to the **New World**. Esquivel and his army established the town of Sevilla la Nueva on Jamaica's north coast. They quickly overpowered the local Taínos and forced them into slavery. In the years that followed, thousands of Taínos died of disease, starvation, or overwork.

The Taíno were known as a gentle people who lived a simple lifestyle. The Spanish had few problems overtaking and enslaving them.

To replace the dwindling Taíno slave population, the Spanish began bringing in slaves from Africa. In only a few decades, the population of the Caribbean had been transformed. By the 17th century, the Taíno, Carib, and other indigenous groups were nearly **exterminated**, the Spanish ruled over the islands, and African slaves were arriving by the thousands.

British settlers focused much of their attention on growing crops that could be sold in Europe. The majority of slaves worked on sugar plantations, where they harvested and processed sugarcane into sugar.

Spanish dominance in the Caribbean was under threat by other European nations. Great Britain, France, Portugal, and the Netherlands were all in competition with Spain for control of New World territories. In 1655, Britain drove the Spanish out of Jamaica. British settlers arrived and began building plantations on the island. Like the Spanish, the British also used slave labor. Many slaves were forced to work in the fields of the British plantations.

In 1672, the Royal African Company was established. This British company specialized in trading slaves. Jamaica became one of the company's main trading centers. The island's slave population grew to about 300,000 as a result. A large number of slaves were able to escape and make their way into the mountains. There, they joined forces with the remaining Taínos. Together, these people, known as Maroons, rebelled against the British. While some were able to secure their freedom through **treaties**, many were captured and shipped to other British colonies.

Slavery remained in Jamaica well into the 19th century. The British slave trade was abolished in 1807, and all slaves in British colonies, including Jamaica, were deemed free in 1838. However, it would not be until 1962 that Jamaica gained its independence from Great Britain.

The Age of Exploration
BY THE NUMBERS

85 percent
Estimated portion of Taínos that were killed by colonists through violence and disease.

1670
Year Britain and Spain signed the Treaty of Madrid, officially recognizing Britain's claim to Jamaica.

January 6
Date the Jamaican town of Accompong holds an annual festival to celebrate the first Maroon treaty.

Between 1655 and 1813, there were 16 slave revolts in Jamaica. These conflicts eventually led to the abolishment of slavery on the island.

POPULATION

Almost 3 million people call Jamaica home. In the past, Jamaica was mainly a **rural** society. Today, however, more than half of the population lives in **urban** centers. This move toward urbanization is partly due to Jamaica's young population. Young people generally find more employment and housing opportunities in urban settings. Jamaica's **median age** is only 29 years.

Kingston is currently home to nearly 1 million people. Portmore, Spanish Town, and Montego Bay are the only other Jamaican cities with populations of more than 100,000. The rest of Jamaica's people are spread out in smaller cities and towns, as well as in more rural settings.

Jamaica has about the same number of men as it does women. **Life expectancy** is 77 years for women and 73 years for men. The country's population is growing very slowly, at less than 1 percent per year. This is mainly because there are more people moving away from the island than there are people **immigrating** to it.

Population BY THE NUMBERS

668 Number of people per square mile in Jamaica in 2019. (258 per sq. km)

937,700 Estimated population of Kingston in 2019.

26 percent Portion of Jamaican population that is aged 14 and under.

Almost 20 percent of Jamaica's population lives below the poverty line. Charities help the poor by providing them with food and health care.

POLITICS AND GOVERNMENT

2006

Year that Portia Simpson-Miller became Jamaica's first female prime minister.

12 Minimum number of members that can be in the Jamaican cabinet, including the prime minister.

18 Age a person must be to vote in Jamaican elections.

Even though Jamaica gained its independence from Britain, it remains part of the **Commonwealth**. Like most Commonwealth nations, Jamaica is both a **democracy** and a **constitutional monarchy**. The country's head of state is the British monarch. The prime minister is the leader of the government.

Jamaica's **legislature**, or parliament, has two houses. The House of Representatives is responsible for creating and passing laws. Its members are elected by the people. The leader of the political party that wins the most seats in an election becomes prime minister. It is the prime minister's job to form a **cabinet**. Together, the prime minister and the cabinet make up the executive branch of the government.

The Senate is the other house in Jamaica's government. It has the right to change or block laws passed by the House of Representatives. Senators are appointed to their posts. The prime minister appoints thirteen senators, while the other eight are recommended by the leader of the opposition party.

The leaders of Commonwealth nations meet every two years to discuss the issues facing their countries. In 2018, Jamaican prime minister Andrew Holness attended the conference in London, England.

CULTURAL GROUPS

Jamaican culture is a colorful blend, created over centuries by the diverse cultural groups who have called the island home. Indigenous, European, and African groups are the most notable through history. Today, the vast majority of Jamaica's population are of African **ancestry**.

There are two distinct Maroon cultures in Jamaica. Each one developed independently from the other. The Leeward Maroons are found in the western Cockpit Country, while the Windward Maroons live in the Blue Mountains area of the east. Maroon towns are allowed to elect their own leaders, known as "colonels," and are considered mostly independent from the rest of Jamaica.

Jamaica's Maroon history is prominently displayed throughout the country. The town of Saint Andrew features a statue of Nanny of the Maroons, one of the best-known leaders of the Maroon rebellions.

Traditional Jamaican music features many African influences. Bands often make use of the djembe, an African drum, in their performances.

Jamaica's official language is English, but the most widely spoken language is Patois, or Jamaican **Creole**. This language mixes English with elements of several West African languages. Patois is just one example of how the Jamaican people held on to their African roots in the face of colonialism.

Another example of the island's African influence can be seen in the uniquely Jamaican religion, Rastafarianism. Like Patois, Rastafarianism grew out of a combination of western and African traditions. Founded in the 1930s, it is a response to the enslavement of Africans throughout history and the need to restore African freedom and power. While only about 1 percent of Jamaicans follow Rastafarianism, it is one of the best-known aspects of Jamaican culture. The most commonly practiced religion in Jamaica is Protestantism.

Jamaican food also represents the meeting of different cultures throughout history. The crops first grown by the island's indigenous peoples remain an important part of Jamaican cuisine. Plantains and coconuts are used to make tarts and pastries similar to those found in Europe. Peppers are the main ingredient in pepperpot soup, a South American stew. African slaves are responsible for Jamaica's national breakfast dish, ackee and saltfish. The African influence can also be tasted in the popular rice and peas dish.

4 Number of Maroon communities in Jamaica today.

#1 Jamaica's ranking as the country with the highest number of churches **per capita**.

3 million
Number of people that speak Patois worldwide.

Followers of Rastafarianism are known for their long dreadlocked hair, which mimics a lion's mane and symbolizes strength.

ARTS AND ENTERTAINMENT

J amaica is known around the world as the home of reggae music. The word "reggae" comes from the Jamaican phrase *rege-rege*, which means rags. Reggae music is known for its raggedy style, as well as its soulful sound. Reggae itself grew out of a style of music called ska, which was developed in Jamaica in the 1950s and 1960s. Today, reggae influences can be heard in Jamaica's dub and dancehall music.

Over the course of his career, Bob Marley sold more than 20 million albums worldwide.

The best-known reggae musician to come out of Jamaica was Bob Marley. Even decades after his death, Marley remains Jamaica's most iconic figure. His songs, which promote messages of peace, love, and unity, are still played all over the world. Several of Marley's children have also become successful reggae musicians. In 1979, his oldest son, Ziggy, started a band called the Melody Makers, with his brother Stephen, and his sisters Cedella and Sharon. Bob's grandsons, Bambaata and Skip Marley, continue the family tradition of making music. Peter Tosh, Jimmy Cliff, and the band Raging Fyah are just a few of the many other Jamaican reggae musicians who have made an impact on popular music.

Raging Fyah was formed in 2002 as a band called Inside Out. It changed its name in 2006, and since then, has gone on to become one of reggae's most promising new acts.

Visual arts are another major part of Jamaican culture. Developed from a mix of Caribbean, African, and European traditions, Jamaican painting and sculpture feature bright colors and vibrant scenes. Struggle and triumph are common themes in Jamaican art. Albert Huie is one of Jamaica's most recognized painters. He is known for painting epic scenes of Jamaican people and the lush Jamaican landscape. One of his paintings was even featured on a Jamaican postage stamp. Edna Manley is Jamaica's best-known sculptor. Born in England, Manley became a champion of Jamaican culture, sculpting works depicting the strength and pride of the Jamaican people. Today, one of Jamaica's top art colleges is named after Manley.

Jamaican writers and poets have worked to preserve and promote Jamaican culture by sharing their stories and experiences. Known as the "mother of Jamaican culture," Louise Bennett-Coverley was a poet who promoted the use of Patois in writing. In fact, she wrote and recited her poetry using Patois. "Miss Lou," as she was sometimes known, was also the author of several folktales and recorded albums of Jamaican folk songs for both adults and children. Other writers who have contributed to Jamaica's literary scene include Nicola Yoon, Lorna Goodison, and Colin Channer.

1993 Year the first Reggae Sumfest, Jamaica's largest music festival, was held in Montego Bay.

8 feet Height of the statue of Miss Lou unveiled in Gordon Town in 2018. (2.4 m)

2014 Year Bob Marley's *Legend* album reached the Billboard Top 10, 30 years after its release

One of Edna Manley's sculptures can be seen on the Kingston waterfront. It was created in 1991 to commemorate 30 years of Jamaican independence.

SPORTS

Watching and participating in sports are popular pastimes in Jamaica. Cricket is a Jamaican passion that grew out of British colonialism. In the past, it was only played by British elites. Today, however, Jamaicans of all backgrounds play cricket. Internationally, Jamaica plays as part of the West Indies team. Known as the Windies, the team consists of the best players from countries including Jamaica, Antigua and Barbuda, Dominica, Guyana, Saint Lucia, Trinidad and Tobago, Barbados, Grenada, and St. Vincent and the Grenadines. Sabina Park in Kingston is Jamaica's major cricket stadium. It seats 20,000 spectators.

In 2007, Jamaica hosted the ICC Cricket World Cup. The Trelawny Stadium was built to host the opening ceremonies.

Soccer has always been popular in Jamaica, but since 1998, it has grown to challenge cricket as the island's favorite sport. That year, the national men's team, known as the Reggae Boyz, qualified for the FIFA World Cup. The country celebrated with a national holiday, and each player was awarded a piece of land by the prime minister. The Reggae Boyz only managed to win one game, but 1998 is remembered as the country's greatest soccer triumph. The national women's team, the Reggae Girlz, qualified for the 2019 FIFA Women's World Cup. It was Jamaica's first time at the tournament.

The Reggae Girlz qualified for the 2019 World Cup by winning against Panama at the CONCACAF Women's Championships in Frisco, Texas, with a score of 4–2.

Jamaica's best-known athlete is often called "the world's fastest man." In 2008, Usain Bolt burst into the spotlight when he won two gold medals in sprinting at the Olympics, setting two new world records at the same time. Bolt then went on to win three gold medals at both the 2012 and 2016 Olympics. While Bolt has retired from track and field events, he still holds world records in the 100m, 200m, and 4x100m sprints.

Jamaica's most beloved athletes are probably its bobsled team. In 1988, the unlikely Caribbean underdogs qualified for the Winter Olympics. Despite their slow times, and even a crash during a race, the Jamaican bobsled team members were among the most popular athletes at the games. They qualified again for each Winter Olympics until 2002. After a 12-year absence, Jamaican bobsledders returned to the Winter Olympics in 2014.

Usain Bolt led the Jamaican men's relay team to victory at the London Olympics in 2012. The team broke its own world record, finishing the race with a time of 36.84 seconds.

Sports
BY THE NUMBERS

25,000 Number of people Trelawny Stadium seats.

9.58 seconds
World record time of Usain Bolt's 100m sprint.

1993 Year the movie *Cool Runnings* was released, recounting the story of the first Jamaican bobsled team.

Mapping Jamaica

We use many tools to interpret maps and to understand the locations of features such as cities, states, lakes, and rivers. The map below has many tools to help interpret information on Jamaica.

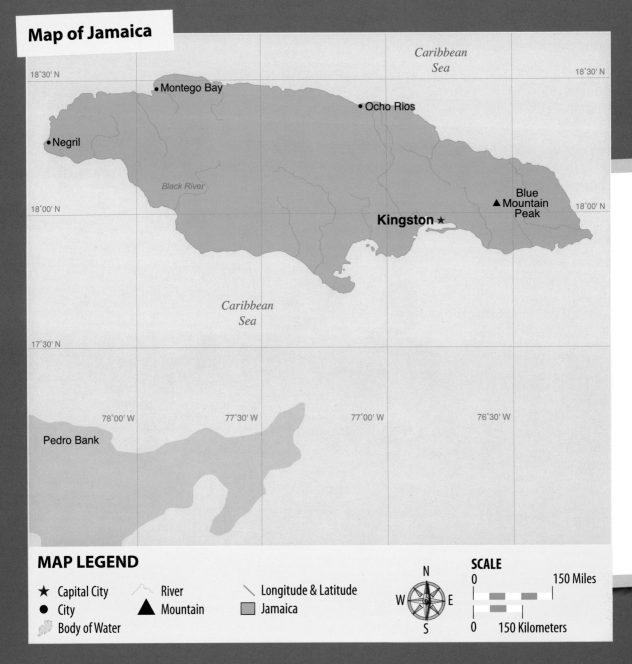

Map of Jamaica

- 18°30' N
- 18°00' N
- 17°30' N

- Montego Bay
- Ocho Rios
- Negril
- Black River
- Kingston ★
- Blue Mountain Peak ▲
- Caribbean Sea
- Caribbean Sea
- Pedro Bank

- 78°00' W
- 77°30' W
- 77°00' W
- 76°30' W

MAP LEGEND

- ★ Capital City
- ● City
- 🌊 Body of Water
- River
- ▲ Mountain
- ╲ Longitude & Latitude
- ▮ Jamaica

N
W — E
S

SCALE
0 — 150 Miles

0 — 150 Kilometers

Mapping Tools

- The compass rose shows north, south, east, and west. The points in-between represent northeast, northwest, southeast, and southwest.

- The map scale shows that the distances on a map represent much longer distances in real life. If you measure the distance between objects on a map, you can use the map scale to calculate the actual distance in miles or kilometers between those two points.

- The lines of latitude and longitude are long lines that appear on maps. The lines of latitude run east to west and measure how far north or south of the equator a place is located. The lines of longitude run north to south and measure how far east or west of the Prime Meridian a place is located. A location on a map can be found by using the two numbers where latitude and longitude meet. This number is called a coordinate and is written using degrees and direction. For example, the city of Kingston would be found at 17°N and 76°W on a map.

Map It!

Using the map and the appropriate tools, complete the activities below.

Locating with latitude and longitude
1. Which mountain is located at 18°N and 76°W?
2. Which natural area is located at 17°N and 78°W?
3. Which city is found at 18°28′N and 77°55′W?

Distances between points
4. Using the map scale and a ruler, calculate the approximate distance between Negril and Ocho Rios.
5. Using the map scale and a ruler, calculate the approximate distance between Kingston and Montego Bay.
6. Using the map scale and a ruler, calculate the approximate length of the Black River.

Quiz Time

Test your knowledge of Jamaica by answering these questions.

1 To which island group does Jamaica belong?

2 What is Jamaica's highest mountain?

3 Which Jamaican port is the main stopping point for cruise ships?

4 What is Jamaica's top export?

5 Who founded the first European settlement in Jamaica?

6 What is Jamaica's median age?

7 Who was Jamaica's first female prime minister?

8 What is the name of the Jamaican Creole language?

9 Who is Jamaica's best-known reggae musician?

10 What is the nickname of the Jamaican national women's soccer team?

ANSWERS

1. Greater Antilles
2. Blue Mountain Peak
3. Falmouth
4. Aluminum oxide
5. Juan de Esquivel
6. 29 years
7. Portia Simpson-Miller
8. Patois
9. Bob Marley
10. Reggae Girlz

Key Words

ancestry: referring to people in one's family or cultural group from past times

archaeologists: scientists who study human history, often by examining ancient objects

bauxite: a type of rock that has high aluminium content

cabinet: a group of politicians selected for specific government jobs

cassava: the starchy root of a tropical tree

colony: a country under control of another

Commonwealth: a group of countries formerly colonized by Great Britain

constitutional monarchy: a system of government in which the powers of a hereditary ruler are limited by a country's constitution and laws

Creole: a language created by blending other languages

democracy: a type of government in which people choose their leaders by voting

earthenware: pottery made from clay and other natural materials

endemic: native and restricted to a certain place

erosion: the gradual removal of rock or soil by rivers, the sea, or the weather

export: goods sold to other countries

exterminated: wiped out

fisheries: waters used for fishing

gross domestic product (GDP): the total value of all the goods and services produced in a country's economy

hurricane belt: an area that experiences frequent hurricanes

immigrating: moving to another country

imported: bought goods from other countries

legislature: a group of people that have the power to make or change laws in a country or area

life expectancy: the length of time a person should be expected to live

mangrove: a swampy coastal forest common in the tropics

median age: the age that half the people in a population are younger than and half are older than

New World: a colonial term for North and South America and the Caribbean

oral: spoken, not written

per capita: for each person

plantations: farm-like settlements common throughout the tropics

plateaus: high, flat areas

remittances: money sent from one country to another

rural: outside of cities or towns

savannas: dry, grassy plains

sinkholes: cavities in the ground caused by water erosion

species: groups of plants or animals with common characteristics

textiles: woven or knit materials

trade winds: nearly constant winds that blow through the tropics

treaties: negotiated agreements

tropical: relating to an area between two lines of latitude, the Tropic of Cancer and the Tropic of Capricorn

urban: in cities or towns

Index

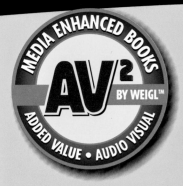

Log on to www.av2books.com

AV² by Weigl brings you media enhanced books that support active learning. Go to www.av2books.com, and enter the special code found on page 2 of this book. You will gain access to enriched and enhanced content that supplements and complements this book. Content includes video, audio, weblinks, quizzes, a slideshow, and activities.

AV² Online Navigation

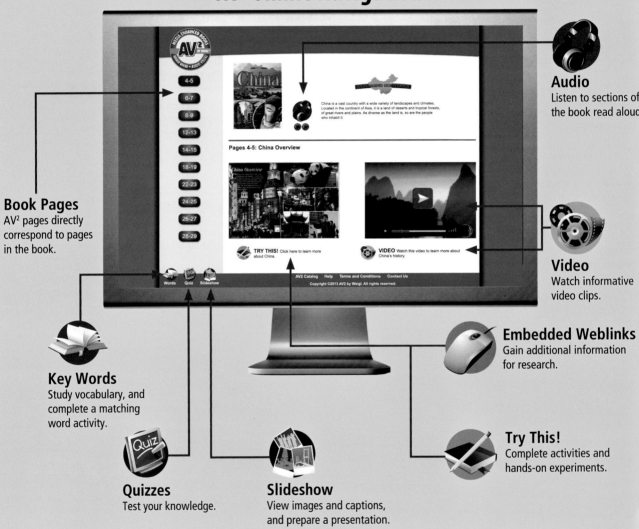

Book Pages
AV² pages directly correspond to pages in the book.

Audio
Listen to sections of the book read aloud

Video
Watch informative video clips.

Embedded Weblinks
Gain additional information for research.

Try This!
Complete activities and hands-on experiments.

Key Words
Study vocabulary, and complete a matching word activity.

Quizzes
Test your knowledge.

Slideshow
View images and captions, and prepare a presentation.

AV² was built to bridge the gap between print and digital. We encourage you to tell us what you like and what you want to see in the future.

Sign up to be an AV² Ambassador at www.av2books.com/ambassador.